CrumbGobbler Press

13451 Wetmore Road
San Antonio, Texas 78247

ISBN 978-0-9795302-1-0
Library of Congress Control Number: 2007930616
Text Copyright © 2007 by Miriam Aronson and Jeff Aronson
Illustration Copyright © 2007 by Downtown Wetmore Press

This book is dedicated to Natalee Aronson.

If you would like additional copies from the *Little Mike and Maddie* series of books, please visit:

www.CrumbGobbler.com

Little Mike and Maddie were so excited.
It was their first motorcycle rally and a big one, too.
Their campground was filled with people who had come to have fun and
go riding in the Black Hills. They were playing ball with some new friends
when Amy called out, "Little Mike! Maddie! Let's go get some pancakes!"
Little Mike and Maddie ran as fast as they could to their cabin.

They loved pancakes, but what they loved most was to jump into the sidecar and zoom down the road with Big Bob and Amy. Big Bob started up the shiny red motorcycle and "Vrumm, vrumm!" They all rode together into town.

WELCOME RIDERS!

SALE TODAY!

T-SHIRTS

HATS

The Leather Stop

LIVE MUSIC

WHEELS

Little Mike and Maddie couldn't believe their eyes when they turned onto Main Street. They had never seen so many motorcycles before! Engines roared. People were noisy and happy. Little Mike saw a girl waving at them and barked, "It's our first motorcycle rally!"

Big Bob parked the motorcycle in the first spot he could find. "The pancake wagon is down the block," he said to Amy with a wink, "but there's lots to see along the way. Let's start with the toy store."

Little Mike loved toy stores. He was so happy when he found a new squeaky duck. Next it was Maddie's turn, but she didn't want to look at toys. She loved to eat and there was food everywhere. The only thing that made her forget for a minute about pancakes was seeing all the other dogs on motorcycles.

"It's our first motorcycle rally!"
Little Mike barked to a fluffy brown dog
riding by. "Mine, too," the dog barked
back. "Welcome to the Black Hills!"
As Little Mike tried on a bandana and
some funny hats, Maddie was getting
hungrier and hungrier. She saw a
man holding a smoked turkey leg and
couldn't resist taking a lick.

"There's Knucklehead Dave's Famous Flapjacks!" said Amy. Maddie raced to the wagon, but Big Bob, Amy and Little Mike stopped to look at a sign. "Hey, there's a dog parade today in Keystone," said Big Bob. "Sounds fun, but we better get Maddie some pancakes first."

It didn't take long for Maddie to gobble everything down so she could have a second helping. Little Mike ate just a couple bites because he was too busy watching the other dogs passing by Knucklehead Dave's wagon.

KIDS JACKETS!

CLASSIC LEATHER

"We're on our way to the parade," barked a tiny dog with shaggy ears, and his friends wagged their tails. "We'll see you there!" barked Little Mike as the three dogs rode away.

By the time Maddie finished eating,
she was so full of pancakes that she
needed some help to get up. She
waddled behind Big Bob and Amy
while Little Mike made squeaky
noises with his new toy.
He was very excited about
going to the dog parade.

BUY 3 - GET 1 FREE!

Suddenly a dog wearing a pretty polka-dot bandana rode by on a pink trike.
Little Mike was sure he'd seen her that morning at the campground.
"Hi!" he barked, but she didn't hear him and the trike rumbled down the street.

Big Bob fired up the shiny red motorcycle and "Vrumm, vrumm!" Just for fun they rode up Main Street and down again past the toy store and the tent with the hats and the pancake wagon and all the motorcycles. Little Mike hoped the dog with the polka-dot bandana might be going to the parade, too.

Out on the highway, Big Bob made the motorcycle go fast.
Little Mike and Maddie loved the wind flapping their ears.
Other motorcycles whizzed by and the riders waved and smiled.
Everyone was enjoying the beautiful day in the Black Hills.

When they got to the town of Deadwood, Little Mike and Maddie forgot all about the dog parade because there were so many fun things to do here, too. First they dressed up in Old West clothes for a family photo. Little Mike and Maddie couldn't believe how funny they looked.

Next they stopped at a gold mine and panned for gold with Big Bob and Amy. It was a good thing they already had their picture taken because Little Mike fell into the creek and got all wet. "Okay, Booger and Dog Breath, it's time to go," Big Bob said with a laugh as Little Mike shook water everywhere.

DEADWOOD GOLD MINE

A winding twisty road carried them past forests and lakes to Hill City. Little Mike and Maddie wagged their tails with excitement when they heard a loud whistle from the steam train just leaving the depot.

"Look at the two dogs in the sidecar!" shouted a red-haired girl. Everyone waved out the windows at Little Mike and Maddie as Big Bob rode alongside the train all the way to Keystone.

It was late when they got into town and they had missed the parade. Most of the other dogs on motorcycles were already leaving. "That's all right," Big Bob said. "Let's get some ice cream."

Maddie didn't mind missing the parade because she was hungry again, and she loved ice cream. She was so busy sniffing the air for yummy things to eat that she didn't see Little Mike standing on the edge of the sidecar.

Little Mike couldn't believe it! The pink trike was stopped right in front of them and there was the dog with the polka-dot bandana. He barked "Hello!" and this time, she heard him. She hopped up from her seat to bark back, but suddenly lost her balance. Oh no!

Little Mike jumped out of the sidecar to save her from tumbling into the street. "Little Mike!" cried Amy as he pulled the dog back into her seat.

Little Mike was glad the dog with the polka-dot bandana was safe and sound, but he didn't feel so happy anymore when the lady driving the trike roared off down the road. She didn't see Little Mike sitting behind her.

What was Little Mike going to do? He saw Maddie barking and Amy waving her arm for the lady to stop as Big Bob chased after the trike. The dog with the polka-dot bandana was nice, but Little Mike wanted to be with his family.

"Don't worry, Amy, we'll catch up with them," shouted Big Bob over the roar of the motorcycle. Maddie kept right on barking. She wanted Little Mike back with her in the sidecar. The lady was going so fast that they lost sight of her around a turn.

"Have you seen a pink trike?" Big Bob asked the park ranger at Mount Rushmore. Maddie was so worried about Little Mike, she didn't notice the four gigantic faces carved into the mountain. "Why, yes," said the man, pointing down the road. "They passed by a few minutes ago."

When Big Bob, Amy, and Maddie had to stop at a tunnel to let some other motorcycles pass by, they fell even more behind. It was all they could do to sit still and wait until it was their turn to ride through the tunnel. How far away was Little Mike now?

Up ahead, Little Mike had lost sight of Big Bob, Amy, and Maddie. As the trike roared into Custer State Park, he hoped a herd of buffalo munching grass might block them so they had to stop. Or maybe the wild burros rubbing their backs on the trees might run across the road. He barked at them, but the buffalo kept right on eating grass and the burros kept right on scratching.

It wasn't until the lady reached the Crazy Horse Memorial that she pulled into a parking space and climbed off the trike. "Where did you come from?" she asked in surprise when she saw Little Mike.

Little Mike wagged his tail, but he wasn't looking at the lady. He heard Big Bob's motorcycle and Maddie's barking coming closer and closer until suddenly, he saw them! When Big Bob pulled up alongside the trike, Little Mike jumped into the sidecar.

AS Amy gave him a huge hug and Maddie licked his face, Little Mike knew they weren't upset with him at all. "Little Mike Saved your dog from falling out of her Seat," Big Bob Said to the lady, and She gave Little Mike a huge hug, too.

"See you back at the campground!" Little Mike barked to the dog with the polka-dot bandana. He was so happy to be together with his family again and he was getting sleepy, too, from their Black Hills adventure.

After supper, Little Mike and Maddie snuggled into their bed. They had missed the dog parade, but the Christmas parade back home was only a few months away. Little Mike nuzzled Maddie. "Good night, Maddie May." Maddie cuddled closer to Little Mike. "Good night, Mikey." It didn't take long for them to fall asleep and dream of the next exciting adventure to come. Vrumm, vrumm . . .